Moths & Butterflies

Charity Parkerson

Punk & Sissy Publications

Copyright

—Warning: This book is intended for readers over the age of 18. Some of my books contain allusions to past abuse and trauma.

Contents

Introduction

IZZIE IS CONTENT WITH her quiet life and secondhand store. She doesn't need more. Until Anna sweeps her away, that is.

A slow economy might have Izzie's store on the brink of bankruptcy, but she still loves the place. Every day, she wakes up knowing she has achieved what she's always wanted. Each day, Izzie also watches the most flawless woman she's ever seen jog past her on her way to work. She never expects the blonde bombshell would notice her, until she does, making Izzie realize her store might not be her biggest dream after all.

For months, Anna has searched for a way to talk to Izzie. When it finally happens, Anna realizes almost immediately she might have made a mistake. Her plans for the future aren't in a small town in Virginia. She's worked tirelessly to achieve bigger things. Izzie makes her question every choice. How can she chase her castle in the sky when Izzie might be the only fantasy she truly needs?

Moths & Butterflies is an FF contemporary romance where two women headed in opposite directions have to choose between love and the future they've each strived to achieve.

Chapter One

THE SOUND OF FEET slapping the pavement had Izzie dropping her gaze to the ground. It was five minutes past eight on the dot. The same as every morning. Just as she did daily, the blonde bombshell stopped at the end of the sidewalk and braced herself on the railing that separated them from the Elizabeth River. She stretched while Izzie watched. Of course, Izzie kept her face straight ahead, as if watching for the ferry, and gawked on the sly. Izzie would never purposely make the other woman uncomfortable, but damn. She was beautiful. With her long blonde hair in a ponytail, and the perfectly toned body Izzie could never achieve, she was the epitome of beauty. No doubt every woman she met hated her on sight. She was tan and had sexy-as-fuck legs. Each day, she jogged past Izzie as she waited for the ferry to carry her to work on the other side of the river. Every day was the same torture. She was a dream Izzie would never have.

Izzie imagined she was likely in the military, since they were a military town. That explained the daily jog and toned body. Not that Izzie knew for sure. They had never spoken beyond the occasional good morning greeting. Izzie was just one of those people who made up entire stories in their mind about everyone she saw. She had a whole life painted for her mystery woman. None of it included anyone like Izzie.

To Izzie's shock, her obsession didn't jog away after her stretch, as usual. Instead, she walked Izzie's way. "You changed your hair."

Izzie's gaze shot toward the woman. Her eyes were the color of a summer's sky. Of course they were. She was freaking perfect.

"Uh. Yeah. I did it last night."

Her walking fantasy filled the spot next to her on the bench. She touched the rainbow-colored locks that were now mixed into Izzie's long, dark hair. "I love it. It looks great. I'm Anna." She held out a hand for Izzie to shake.

Izzie accepted. A nervous laugh burst from her. "Ha. I'm Izzie. Izzie and Anna. How cute?" She wanted to punch herself in the face. Izzie immediately tried swerving away from her dumbass comment. "Thanks. About the hair, I mean. It's nothing like your gorgeous hair, but I tried." Goddamn. Could she sound any more empty-headed? Anna would probably change the route for her morning run after this ridiculous encounter. She probably thought Izzie was insane.

Anna's eyes shone bright laughter. "I think it's great. The Navy would never let me get away with those bright colors, but I've always wanted to try it."

Navy. She had called it. Izzie nodded. "I own my own business, so I get to do what I want. How long have you been in the Navy?"

"Seven years. What kind of business do you own?"

Izzie saw the ferry approaching in the distance. She already dreaded the end of their conversation. "It's a secondhand store across the river in the market district: Moths &

Butterflies. I sell gently used clothing and some antiques. Things like that."

Anna smiled. "I'll have to come check that out sometime. That's a great name for a secondhand store."

Izzie beamed. "Right? My aunt kind of scoffed at it when I told her what I planned to name the place, but I think it fits. You never know what you'll find. It might be a treasure or might only be a treasure to you: Moths & Butterflies."

The longer they talked, the less nervous Izzie felt. Anna was every bit as wonderful as Izzie had always hoped. "I'd love for you to stop by. The shop opens at ten every morning except Sunday. I'm closed then. Oh, and I close every day at seven."

Anna nodded. "Sounds great. I'm sure I can make it by sometime within that timeframe." Anna's gaze slid toward the approaching ferry. "It looks like I should get back to my run and let you catch your ride. It was nice talking to you."

"You too." Izzie's smile was genuine. She was beyond happy. Izzie hadn't thought they would ever actually meet. Now she had a name. Her day was made. She could die happy now.

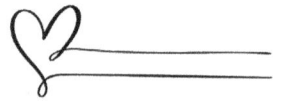

Anna had run the same path for months, since the day she was stationed in Virginia. Not a day went by where Izzie wasn't there. Each morning, they greeted each other. Every day, Anna tried to get Izzie to speak to her, but she couldn't think of a way to start a conversation. Izzie never looked at her directly. It was hard to make friends as an adult.

The new hair color gave Anna the perfect opening. She hadn't wanted to miss her shot. Now that they had finally spoken, Anna was so glad she had gone out on a limb. Izzie seemed genuinely fantastic.

She made the jog back to her apartment, feeling buoyed by the entire experience. The happiness carried her through the day. Since moving to Virginia, she had been crazy lonely. All her friends were back in Texas, and everything she did for fun felt so far away. By the time she made it home for the night, her joy had faded a hair. Her apartment was still empty. It would be another night of eating alone. Anna took another shower to wash away the sweat of the day. As she headed for her bedroom, she caught sight of the red numbers on her bedroom clock. She still had time.

For a full minute, Anna stared at nothing as the idea grew larger. A smile exploded across her face. She tossed aside her towel and rushed around the room, grabbing clothes as she went. Anna was dressed and ready in under fifteen minutes. She was out the door in under twenty. Luck was on her side as she left her apartment building. The ferry approached the dock. She ran for it and made it to the gate just as they set out the ramp. Impatience had her pressing her hands against her knees to stop them from bobbing after she showed her monthly pass and found a seat.

Normally, Anna enjoyed the ferry. It was rarely packed, and she loved the water. It was a peaceful way to travel. Tonight, she resented the slow traverse across the water. She kept checking her watch. When the ferry finally docked on the other side, it hit her she had no idea where she was going. Anna dug her phone from her back pocket and quickly Googled the store. Relief washed over her when she saw it was only two streets away. With directions in hand, she headed that way. Anna prayed she didn't look like a crazy person.

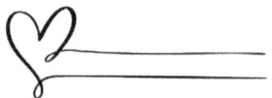

It had been another slow day. Depression settled into Izzie's soul as she went through the motions at five minutes until closing time. Moths & Butterflies had been such a huge dream realized for her. Izzie needed to work for herself. She hadn't been built to have a boss. But a slow economy had hurt businesses everywhere and Izzie had taken one hell of a hit. She got up and tried her ass off every day, but things weren't getting better. In her heart, she knew she could call her brother and he would bail out her business. She didn't want to do that. Shane had already given up everything for her. Izzie couldn't ask for more. This was her mess. She would have to figure it out.

"Do you need help with that?"

Izzie startled, sending baskets flying in every direction. She had been searching for a spot for some awesome baskets she bought at a yard sale when Anna had gotten the drop on her. "Holy shit."

Musical laughter filled the air. Anna bent to help her scoop up the mess. "I'm sorry. I thought you heard me come in."

Wow. She looked amazing. With form-fitting jeans and tank top that accentuated her curves, Anna was stunning. She smelled great too. "Sorry. I guess I was lost in thought."

"It's okay. I get lost in my head all the time too."

They stood, holding the baskets. Izzie couldn't look away from Anna's blue eyes. Silence grew between them. Finally, Anna smiled. "I should admit, I waited until closing time."

Izzie's eyebrows rose. "Really? Why?"

Another melodic laugh fell from Anna's perfect lips. "Um. I don't want to sound crazy."

"Why not? I'm crazy."

Anna's eyes danced with laughter at Izzie's unexpected admission. "Okay. Well, here it goes, then. Everyone I know is back in Texas and it was really great talking to you this morning. I thought, if you're up to it, maybe I can take you to dinner."

Izzie had never considered what would happen if her dream woman asked her to dinner. That seemed like such a far-fetched scenario. But here they were, and Izzie's thoughts were all over the place. Anna was in the Navy and jogged every day. Izzie would probably look like a cow next to her, eating.

Anna shifted from foot to foot. "I understand if you don't feel comfortable going to dinner with a stranger. It looks like all the food trucks are out tonight. We could grab something and go our separate ways if you feel uncomfortable."

"I'd love to grab something to eat with you," Izzie said, rushing to fix any damage her slow brain caused.

Anna's giddy-looking smile had Izzie sighing inside. Maybe Anna could be a friend, if nothing else. It wasn't like Izzie couldn't use one of those too.

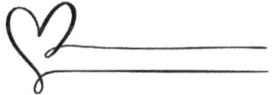

Food trucks littered the cobblestone street. Anna walked the path with Izzie at her side. She smelled nice—like something a mixture of sweet and sultry. Anna found herself moving closer. Each time, she held her breath and waited. Izzie didn't move away. A park bench emptied, and Anna rushed Izzie toward it before anyone else could steal it.

They'd been walking for nearly an hour, just waiting for their chance.

Izzie laughed as Anna nearly launched herself at the bench, cutting off a group of teenagers.

"Age before beauty, bitches," Anna muttered under her breath, making Izzie laugh harder.

To her delight, Izzie sat mere inches from her. "This has been so much fun. I can't tell you the last time I just enjoyed myself. The shop has taken a hit lately with tourism slowing down. I've been so focused on that, I haven't let myself enjoy anything. So, for all that rambling, thank you."

"Please don't thank me. Like I said earlier, I don't really have anyone here. It's been kind of lonely coming home to an empty apartment every night." Anna didn't know why she had admitted that. Izzie had gorgeous hazel eyes. She looked kind and Anna imagined everyone always told her everything. Plus, Anna was simply a southern girl, and everyone told their business to everyone else in the south.

"You said you're from Texas, right?"

Anna nodded. "Born and raised."

"You don't have an accent."

A smile exploded across Anna's face. "Good. I've worked really hard to lose it. Nothing against an accent," Anna rushed to add. "But I went to school for broadcasting, and one teacher made sure I understood that a southern twang wouldn't win me any job offers."

"Broadcasting? That sounds amazing." Izzie sounded truly interested. She didn't stop there. "I can see you doing something like that. You're gorgeous. You should be in front of a camera." She immediately blushed and looked away.

Anna was fascinated. Women complimented women all the time with zero shame. Anna had to know. "So, rainbow hair. Does that mean..."

Izzie didn't look at her. "Yep. Alphabet mafia all the way." She sounded exactly like she expected to be rejected.

"Great. Me too."

Izzie's gaze shot to hers. Her expression screamed shock. "There's literally no way."

Anna couldn't stop the laugh that burst from her. "Why? A military woman out to get a job in sportscasting doesn't sound like she'd be gay? Not that I'm generalizing. That's just literally me." Anna couldn't stop laughing. Izzie's shock was totally worth outing herself.

After a moment, Izzie cleared her throat. "It's not that. You're just..." She gestured wildly at Anna from head to toe. "Perfect. Like, the epitome of what I think every man would want."

Anna pulled a face before she could stop it. "*Ew*. Why would anyone want one of those?"

The loud laugh that burst from Izzie warmed her chest. "Well." Izzie blinked for a second. "Well," she said again. "This has been enlightening."

"It has. See me again."

Izzie chuckled. It sounded nervous. "I haven't recovered from my last shock. Give me a second."

Anna opened her mouth to apologize.

"I'd love to see you again," Izzie said suddenly, stopping Anna from embarrassing herself.

A smile exploded across Anna's face. "Okay."

Izzie's smile matched hers. "Okay."

"It's a date."

At Anna's words, Izzie's smile faltered a little. "A date? No pressure."

Anna shook her head at Izzie's nervous-sounding claim. It was like the woman didn't know she was an absolute goddess with the sexiest curves Anna had ever seen. Next time, Anna would do better at making Izzie feel as beautiful as she was. Izzie would see. Anna could be a charmer when she tried.

Chapter Two

To say Izzie was a complete
mess of nerves would be a vast
understatement. She had changed
outfits a dozen times before landing
on a flowing skirt and peasant
blouse. Izzie wished she had asked if
she needed to dress a certain way.
She felt like she was back in high
school, asking her friends what they
planned to wear. Izzie rolled her eyes

at her thoughts. She was an adult. For once, she could act like it.

The doorbell rang, immediately disproving that theory. She squealed like a teen. Izzie had been half terrified of being stood up, but no. Anna was really there. With a deep breath for courage, she squared her shoulders and opened the door. Izzie immediately lost her breath. In a form-fitting red dress that stopped halfway down the thighs of her long legs, Anna was stunning. She had definitely stolen Izzie's ability to speak. There was no way this beautiful woman wanted her.

"Hey. You look gorgeous."

Izzie tried calming her racing heart. "You too." That was an understatement. "I didn't think to ask where we were going, so I didn't know how to dress." She eyed Anna's tall heels. "I think I'm underdressed."

"Not at all. I was nervous and overdid it."

Anna always confused her. There was no way she didn't know she was a million miles out of Izzie's league. "I can never tell when you're joking."

Confusion filled Anna's features before immediately clearing. She made a dismissive motion. "Come on. I got us reservations."

With a shake of her head, trying to clear it, Izzie grabbed her purse. "I can't wait." She stepped out into the hallway of her apartment building and pulled the door closed. On the way to the elevator, they kept exchanging glances. Slowly, Izzie's nervousness was replaced by something else. A realization creeped closer. Anna was truly interested in her. Just the thought made her weak. As they rode the elevator down, their pinkies touched. Izzie bit her bottom lip to keep from smiling like an idiot. Then the door slid open, setting them free into a crowded world. They headed out. Anna led her to a small sedan. It was a little sporty-looking and red, which suited Anna. There wasn't a single head, male or female, that didn't turn to look when Anna walked past. For nowhere near the first time, Izzie wondered how it felt to be so flawless. It had to be wonderful.

At the restaurant, a man scrambled to open the door for Anna. He begrudgingly held it for Izzie too. Part of Izzie was proud as hell Anna was with her. Another part of her recognized everyone likely thought they were only friends, and she was the friend they sent their wingmen to handle. It was disheartening and left her feeling deflated.

Then they were seated across from each other, and Anna's attention never wavered from her. "The other night, I feel like I talked too much and didn't let you say anything. You know where I'm from, what I majored in, and several other things. I didn't let you tell me about yourself."

"Well." Izzie squared her shoulders and racked her brain. She didn't really know where to start.
"My family is from Pennsylvania, originally. Then they moved to L.A. for a while for my dad's job and had me. Then my dad passed and my mom kind of shut down. My older brother took over my care until he couldn't any longer. So I moved to Pennsylvania with my aunt."

"That's a lot for a kid."

Izzie shrugged. "I don't really remember much about either of my parents now, and my brother is absolutely amazing. Like, for real, a superstar. I also really adore my aunt and visiting her, so I was kind of excited to live here. She owns this tiny bookstore." Izzie didn't know why she spared no details. Anna looked interested, and she simply kept talking. "It's one of those places that buys old books from customers for store credit. Paperbacks are always stacked to the ceiling. I love the place. The moment I was old enough to work, I jumped right in just to be near all the old books. That's what made me fall in love with secondhand items."

"And now you own your own store."

A sad smile touched Izzie's lips. "For now."

Anna cocked her head to one side. "What do you mean?"

Izzie made a helpless gesture. "So many stores in the marketplace are going under. Tourism just isn't what it used to be with the economy in shambles. If things don't pick up." Izzie shrugged. She couldn't say the words. A life without her store didn't sound like much of a life. She had no idea what she would do with herself without it.

Anna reached across the table and set her hand on Izzie's forearm. "I'm sorry. No one should have to face giving up their dream."

Damn. It was as if Anna stared into her soul and saw her. Izzie didn't know where this night was headed. No matter what, though, she truly felt like she had made a friend. That was more than she had a week ago.

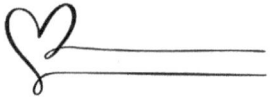

Dinner was perfect. Their conversation never stilted. Izzie's eyes gave away her every thought, and they were gorgeous. She was truly beautiful inside and out. Anna had intentionally waited until Saturday night for their date since Izzie's store was closed on Sunday. Thankfully, it had been easy to convince her to come back to Anna's place for a movie and dessert.

"I wish I had your balance. I've never been able to wear heels."

Anna unlocked her front door and responded over her shoulder. "It's probably just the brand you've tried. I have a pair I guarantee you could wear."

Izzie chuckled. "I seriously doubt that."

With a wave for her to follow, Anna headed for her bedroom. "Come on. I need help with this zipper anyway. No way in hell can I stay in this dress all night."

"No problem." Izzie didn't hesitate to follow Anna inside her bedroom.

Anna opened her closet before flipping her hair aside and exposing the zipper to Izzie. "I really appreciate it. While I can just peel it off, I hate doing that. The zipper always tries ripping out my hair that way."

Izzie slid the zipper down and immediately turned away.

Anna hid a smile as she kicked off her shoes. She peeled off her dress and put her shoes away without bothering to get dressed. Seriously, they were both women. It was a bit funny to her the way Izzie tried so hard not to look. She found the shoes she had mentioned.

"Here. Try these." She pulled them from the box and kneeled. Izzie kicked off her sandals and allowed Anna to help her into the heels. Once she had them on, Anna straightened while still holding Izzie's hand to steady her. "There. Take a step."

While wearing a look of sheer terror, Izzie took a step. She immediately stumbled. Anna caught her. Izzie roared with laughter. Anna couldn't look away. Their faces were inches apart. Anna tightened her hold. The laughter died on Izzie's lips. Her expression shifted as her gaze dropped to Anna's mouth. Anna tentatively touched her lips to Izzie's. A heartbeat passed. Then heat exploded between them. Izzie kicked the shoes aside and came back for more. Anna tugged at Izzie's shirt until Izzie let her have it.

Anna hadn't planned this. She had wanted to move slowly, but she immediately had Izzie out of her bra, and it was out of her control. A moan slipped from her when Izzie's breasts spilled out. She was every bit as beautiful and fantastic as Anna imagined. Anna wasted no time getting her into bed. She might have actually shoved her down, but Izzie didn't complain, and Anna had never wanted anyone as badly. She worshipped the breasts that had teased her all night in that peasant blouse. Izzie took it. An evil smile tugged at Anna's lips. She was either a pillow princess or nervous as hell. Either way, Anna was all the way in. She had her hand up Izzie's skirt before Izzie could complain. When she found her soaking wet, Anna knew that complaint would never come. She massaged her through her panties, trying to get her to the point of letting Anna fully undress her.

Anna kissed her way down Izzie's body, coaxing her out of her panties as she went. The moment she could, Anna struck. She went down on her without holding back. The sound Izzie made had Anna fighting a wicked laugh. Izzie was too sweet. Anna wasn't. Her whole life, she had known what she wanted and didn't stop until it was hers. Anna had been watching Izzie for too long. Now that she had her, she would hear her scream.

"No."

Anna lost her breath. She immediately froze. Whatever Izzie wanted, she would honor.

"I want to taste you too."

Relief poured through Anna. She quickly shimmied out of her underwear and then yanked her further down the bed so she could straddle her face properly. A squeal of laughter escaped Izzie. It died the moment she had a mouth full of pussy. Izzie became a different person. Anna could barely focus on eating Izzie. Izzie had her tongue in there like it was her favorite ice cream. Anna's eyes rolled back in her head. She couldn't stop herself from humping Izzie's face. The closer she got to the edge, the more Anna got into her end of things. She licked and sucked like she was the one feeling the pleasure.

Anna's muscles tightened. She fought to focus. Then her entire body shook, and Izzie didn't stop. Anna was simply crying out her pleasure while face deep in Izzie's crotch. Determination overcame her. She had to make Izzie come every bit as hard. Anna didn't stop or switch positions. She didn't dare make a single move that would cause Izzie to lose the progress she had made. When Izzie's pussy twitched and her body shook beneath Anna, only then did Anna feel fully satisfied.

While Izzie still visibly tried gathering her wits, Anna kissed her.

She wanted Izzie to stay and hold her. No one ever held her. She was that strong, independent woman who didn't need anyone, but she wanted Izzie. As if Izzie read her mind, she grabbed a handful of blanket and tucked it around them. Their tongues went back to playing. Sometimes, there were no words. It had been a wonderful night. It felt like the beginning of something beautiful.

Chapter Three

SEVERAL TIMES, IZZIE STOPPED mid-project and touched her hot cheeks. She had barely left Anna's bed all weekend. Izzie had been shameless and needy. She didn't regret a goddamn thing. Still, she felt a bit out of sorts. Anna wanted her. Holy shit, was Anna's body freaking remarkable. Izzie had never enjoyed touching anyone so much. Not that she had a hell of a lot of experience. She had bought this store at nineteen—with all the audacity of a teenager. Izzie hadn't known shit about owning a business. All she knew was she had to work. This was what she wanted to do, and her brother had been willing to finance her startup. It still blew her away he had agreed to let her do this. She hadn't been a complete disaster at first. Now it was a different story. Izzie was failing dismally and pride kept her from running to Shane.

Poor Shane. He had been her keeper all her life. Shane never complained. In fact, he acted as if her happiness mattered more than anything in the world to him. She didn't deserve him. Her thoughts continued their wild swing between elation and depression. Why had she met this amazing woman when Izzie had literally nothing to offer but a failing business? The sex had been off the charts, but that was hardly enough to hang on to someone like Anna.

Hands covered her eyes, sending her heart racing into her throat. "Guess who?"

Izzie turned and claimed Anna's mouth. Fuck. She would take any amount of time she could get. This woman was freaking awesome.

Anna chuckled against her lips. "Did you miss me?"

"God, so much. Isn't that crazy? Am I being crazy? I don't want to seem needy. Oh, gosh. I'm so bad at this. Can we start this conversation over?" Her shoulders fell. "I want to be sexy and savvy too."

Anna cupped her face and kissed the tip of her nose. "You're perfect."

Izzie had been so excited to see Anna, it hadn't occurred to her it was super early. "Aren't you supposed to be on base or something?"

Anna shrugged. "Not really. I'm hitting the end of my career. Pretty soon... retirement. Yay!"

"You're retiring?" Izzie was fascinated. She knew next to nothing about the military.

Anna made a dismissive gesture. "That's how I'm looking at it. My contract is ending, and I have my college degree now. It's time to move on."

Izzie shifted from foot to foot. She knew she shouldn't let herself get attached. Anna wasn't from here. She probably had already started packing to go back home. "What will you do now?"

"I've been sending out resumes all morning for various broadcasting positions. We'll see."

That didn't make Izzie feel better. She didn't say the jobs were here. "That sounds wonderful."

Anna shrugged. "Anyhow, I was free, so I thought I'd come hang out and help. If that's okay with you, obviously."

Izzie shook off the worry. Anna was here now. "Yes. Of course. I'm always thrilled to see you."

Anna stole another kiss and then went to work next to her like they had worked together for years. Izzie was scared as hell for her heart. There was no going back now. When Anna left, it would break her.

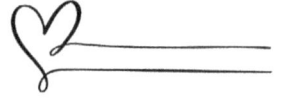

Anna's insides shook. She hadn't truly known how to approach the topic of a career change with Izzie. She shouldn't have waited so long to approach her. They could have had months together. In her defense, Izzie could have shot her down and then Anna would have been forced to change her entire morning routine. There was no way Anna could have known she would feel so much so fast or have such a hard time staying away, but fuck. It had been the best weekend. Anna still hadn't stopped picturing watching Izzie riding her strap. Her nipples hardened just thinking about it. But Izzie had a life here and a store she loved. Anna didn't stand much of a chance of keeping her.

"Were you hopping all day? With the wine festival going on."

Izzie kept her gaze on her hands as she rehung clothes. "Not especially. People aren't really looking to buy secondhand items while tasting wine." Izzie shrugged. There was something about her body language.

Anna couldn't take it. She snagged a nearby rocking chair and sat, giving Izzie her full attention. "Would you like to talk about it?"

Izzie blew out a sigh and grabbed the step stool she had been using. She pulled it close and sat. Her eyes looked sad. "I really love this place." A mixture of pain and happiness filled her voice. "When I first opened, I was so proud of myself, even though

Shane paid for everything. Still, I was setting out into the world and doing what I love. Well, I told you everything is shutting down around here. The lack of foot traffic has me fighting my ass off to keep the doors open, and I'm starting to think I should bow out gracefully before I'm sitting in bankruptcy court. I don't know what to do. Honestly, I can't even picture myself in a nine-to-five job. I'd lose my mind."

Damn. Izzie was so unique. Anna couldn't see her working a regular job. It would crush her spirit. They would probably make her keep a natural hair color. Everything about Izzie appealed to Anna. She was such a light. Anna couldn't watch her be extinguished.

"Have you talked to Shane?"

Izzie pulled a horrified face. "Absolutely not. Shane has already sold his soul to do as much for me as he has. I know that sounds dramatic, but he actually gave away his entire life to make sure I've always had what I need. So, I know he can afford to help, but he shouldn't have to, and how long will that money last before I need even more? I can't do that to him. Unless a miracle happens, I don't imagine I'll last much longer."

That broke Anna's heart. She leaned forward and took Izzie's hands. Anna held Izzie's stare. "You're so amazing. I know there's nothing I can say to make things easier, but I'm here. Anytime you want to unload on me, or cry it out, you've got me." She hated that Izzie had to know this was temporary too. Even if she didn't land a job in her chosen career field, eventually, Anna would have to go back to Texas.

Izzie scooted closer and touched her lips to Anna's.

Anna's eyes burned at the sweetness of the kiss. Her lips parted and Izzie took full advantage. She swept inside and curled her tongue around Anna's. Anna's entire body reacted. She hadn't been this happy in a long time. Her phone rang, interrupting them.

Anna pulled away. "Damn. Give me a minute." She dug through her purse and found her phone. Anna didn't recognize the number, but she still answered. She had too many resumes floating around in the world to ignore an unknown number.

"Hello?"

"May I speak to Anna Lively?"

She didn't recognize the man's voice. "This is she."

"Oh, good. Anna, this is Ronald Wright with CDTV out of New Orleans. I have your resume in front of me and I'd like to go over a few things if you have a moment."

Excitement shot through her. A huge smile stretched her lips, but she tried to stay professional. "Of course. Whatever you need."

"Great. It says here you were a sideline reporter for Navy football. Correct?"

"Yes, sir."

"Do you happen to have any clips for us to view?" He paused for half a second. "Oh, wait. I see you've attached links. Give me a second."

Anna chewed on her thumbnail and held Izzie's stare. Izzie looked curious as hell.

"Ms. Lively?"

"Yes."

"Good. I didn't lose you. This damn new phone system they've had installed is always disconnecting everyone. Anyhow, I glanced at a few clips and wonder if you'd be willing to do an in-person interview?"

Anna blinked. She couldn't believe it. Anna had literally just started sending out resumes that morning. "Yes, of course. I'm in Virginia, so I would need to book a flight."

"I understand. Hold on."

Anna listened to him clicking around.

"Okay. It looks like there's a flight out at seven tonight. Do you think you could make that?"

She checked her watch. It would be tight but doable. "Yes, sir."

"Okay. I'll book that. A driver will pick you up and drop you at a nearby hotel. We can meet at eight a.m. The driver will pass along all the details."

It took everything Anna had not to squeal like a teen. CDTV had been her first choice. Not only was it closer to her parents, but they had a spot open in her specific field: sportscasting.

"I'll gather my things and see you then. Thank you for the opportunity, Mr. Wright."

"Absolutely. You know, I was a Navy man too. I look forward to meeting you."

"That's great. I look forward to meeting you as well. See you soon."

The phone clicked in Anna's ear and the squeal won. "Oh, my God. That was Ronald Wright with CDTV in New Orleans. They have a sportscaster position open and they're flying me out tonight to interview in the morning. Holy shit. I have to go pack a bag."

Izzie stood. "Come on. I'll drive you to the airport."

She was fucking fantastic. Even though this job would take Anna away, she still offered to help. "Thank you. This has just always been my biggest dream."

Izzie nodded. Understanding was all Anna saw in her eyes. "I totally get it. I've been there. Now let's go land you this job."

Anna stopped her before she could head for the door. One thing first. She captured Izzie's lips and took the kiss she wanted. Whatever happened, she would do her best to hang on to Izzie as long as possible. Anna couldn't get enough of this happiness.

Chapter Four

WHILE ANNA STAYED IN New Orleans two days longer than first thought, Izzie had time to think. It was more than obvious Anna had the job. Anna hadn't said it yet, but Izzie saw the writing on the wall. They wouldn't ask her to stay longer for nothing. Two days of doing nothing but thinking allowed Izzie to make a few decisions. First, she had to sell her store. It was time. Right now, if she sold and auctioned all her stock, she could make a profit. The longer she waited, the less that was the case. Second, she would take whatever time she had with Anna and be grateful for it. She could harden her heart and enjoy this as the fling it was. Just like with her shop, not everything had to be permanent. Maybe all these changes would lead to bigger and better things. She already had a few ideas that had her feeling excited all over again about the future. Anything was better than the depression she had been living with. It was time to pick herself up and find a new sense of self. She was young. Everything was temporary.

Unfortunately, Izzie's entire plan had to start with a call to her brother. Izzie couldn't sell the store he had paid for without talking to him about it first. There was no time like the present while she waited for Anna's plane to land. She tapped her fingers on the steering wheel and stared at nothing while listening to the phone ring.

"Hello?"

"Hey, big brother."

"What's wrong? You're using that fake chipper voice I hate. The one where you don't want me knowing what's going on."

Izzie smiled. Shane had always been the best big brother in whole world and knew her better than anyone. He was her brother but might as well be her father, and yet he was also her friend. Shane meant the world to her. Now that she heard his voice, Izzie wanted to kick herself for not calling about this sooner. He had always been her rock. Now was no different.

She cleared her throat and tried not to cry. "Oh, you know. The economy and all that. I have to sell the store." Izzie said the words quickly before she lost her nerve.

A heavy silence fell between them.

Izzie couldn't take it. "I met someone, though. She's incredibly beautiful and so, so nice. You'd love her. She's in the—"

"I don't want you to give up your dream."

Izzie snapped her teeth together at the interruption. Shane said the words so calmly that it made reality that much heavier. "It's not what I want either, but it's time for me to be realistic."

"Give me a number. I won't let you lose the shop. You should've called sooner if you're struggling."

"No." Even Izzie heard the determination in her voice. "I don't want to sit in that store and play owner—like a little girl—while my brother foots the bill. If you keep this funded, I'll always know I'm not really succeeding. I don't know how to explain what I'm trying to say.

But I just need to know I'm doing it and I'm not. It's time for me to pivot and find a new way to feel like a regular adult who can function independently."

For a moment, Shane didn't respond. Finally, he sighed. "Have you made a plan? The money from the sale won't hold you forever."

"I know. I'm still working out the kinks. Aunt Reina once asked me to go into business with her, running the bookstore as co-owners. I've been thinking about how she could double her business by selling her books online too. Maybe I could get that going for her and not be stuck doing something I hate."

"You know I'm always proud of you, right?"

Izzie smiled. "I know."

"You know you can always call me for help, right?"

"I know."

"So you met someone nice?"

Izzie's smile got even bigger. "Yeah. Her name is Anna. She's in the Navy."

Shane chuckled. "I never pictured you with a stud."

A huff burst from Izzie. "Way to stereotype. I have to get a picture of her, so you can eat those words." As if coming to her rescue, Izzie spotted Anna heading her way. She quickly snapped a pic of her and texted it to Shane. "She's walking toward me. I just sent you a picture."

Shane released a low whistle. "Damn, Izzie. Good catch."

Izzie beamed with pride. She wished like hell she could actually keep Anna. Her chest hurt. Life would be extra lonely soon when she didn't even have the shop any longer... or Anna.

"I guess since she's about to reach me, I should let you go."

"Okay. I love you and keep me posted."

"Love you too. I will. Bye."

"Bye."

Izzie disconnected the call and picked up the roses from the passenger seat she had bought Anna.

Anna waved.

Izzie waved back. Her happiness grew bigger by the moment, seeing Anna's bright smile.

Anna climbed into the passenger seat. "Hey."

Izzie handed her the roses. "Hey. How was your trip?"

"Awww." Anna didn't answer. She moved across the console and claimed Izzie's mouth. The pressure in Izzie's chest eased. Whatever happened, she would treasure every second. Izzie had never expected to have this much.

Anna pulled away and wiped her lipstick from Izzie's lips. "I missed you."

God, her heart. It was in danger. "I missed you too. Tell me everything."

Anna sat back and put on her seatbelt. "Well, they didn't make it easy. I ended up having to interview with three different people and Ronald twice. They decided I wasn't a good fit for the TV station."

"Oh no." Even though that was good news for Izzie, she wanted Anna to have her dream.

Anna flashed her a huge grin. "They decided I wasn't a fit for the nightly news, but New Orleans wants me for sideline reporter for their hockey team!"

"Shut up." Izzie was stunned. Anna looked too happy for Izzie to be anything but happy for her. "Oh, my God. That's awesome!"

Anna practically bounced in her seat. "I don't start until a week before the season begins, which is in two months. But that's perfect since I have to finish out my contract with the Navy and find a place in New Orleans. There's just so much to do."

Izzie pulled from the passenger pickup lot and into traffic. Keeping her eyes on the road saved her from hiding her expression. It was really happening. Anna happily spoke of leaving her.

Izzie had to say something to save her sanity. "While you were gone, I made some decisions too. I finally called Shane."

"Does he plan to help you keep the store open?" There was something odd in Anna's tone. But Izzie probably read too much into everything since she silently died inside.

"He offered, but you know that's not what I want. I just called because I needed to know he wouldn't be upset if I put the store up for sale."

Anna didn't respond right away. Finally, she stroked Izzie's arm. "Is that really what you want?"

Was it? She had no clue anymore. "I don't know, but it's reality."

"Oh, babe. I feel like such an ass. I've been sitting here, going on and on about landing this job. Meanwhile, you need me and I'm just... I don't even know."

Izzie looked her way. "No. Don't do that." She went back to watching the road. "You're amazing and wonderful and everything I've ever wanted. This is your dream, and I want it for you. It won't be a total loss for me. After I sell the store and auction all my merchandise, I'll have a great-looking savings account. That should get me by until I'm on my feet. In fact, that frees time for me to come visit you in New

Orleans." As she said the words, Izzie could have bitten her tongue. It was entirely possible Anna wouldn't want to continue things once she moved. Long distance was hard and likely doomed to fail. Izzie just couldn't handle losing her business and Anna in one fell swoop. She pulled into the parking lot of Anna's complex.

"Come inside. I need a shower. Then we can order dinner and talk about it. I've been doing some thinking too."

Aw, fuck. Anna sounded so serious. It seemed Izzie would get that all-in-one-blow hit after all. "Okay." She tried hard to keep her voice steady. "I'd already planned to not let you out of my sight."

A sexy chuckle fell from Anna's lips. "Yeah. You're not getting away from me."

All thought flew out the window. Goosebumps rose on Izzie's skin at the sexual promise in Anna's tone. Her nipples hardened. She already felt Anna between her thighs. Izzie followed her inside with her heart in her throat. As much as Izzie wanted to pounce, that wasn't her style. Thankfully, Anna had no problem being the aggressive one. The moment they were closed inside the apartment, Anna was on her. She pushed Izzie against the closed front door and set her on fire with her kiss. Anna was strong, capable, and sexy. She looked like a beautiful angel. In reality, she was a fucking lion. Izzie felt like prey. She loved it. Anna set her free. It was empowering being so openly wanted by a goddess like Anna. Anna always made her feel like she was the sexiest, most desired woman alive—like Anna couldn't see anyone except her. Izzie had never felt this way. She wanted to own her.

Anna's hand was inside Izzie's panties before she even felt her clothes loosen. She dipped a finger inside Izzie, wetting it before circling Izzie's clit. Izzie sucked in a breath of air so hard, she nearly choked. Anna's mouth moved to her neck while her fingers never stopped moving.

Izzie's hips moved. It was out of her control. Tiny whimpers escaped her as she rode Anna's hand. Fuck. Anna got her so hot, so fast. She could hear how wet she was. Izzie might have been embarrassed if she wasn't in heaven. Anna was perfect. She kept the pressure right and didn't change positions. Her finger played and moved until Izzie held Anna's hips in a death grip, praying she didn't stop. With her eyes squeezed closed and her stomach muscles clenched, Izzie focused everything on those moving fingers. The coil in her stomach wound tighter and tighter. Desperate sounds escaped her. Then her pussy clenched and pulsed, and her knee jerked, nearly taking her to the floor.

Anna didn't stop fingering her until the last spasm passed. Then her mouth found Izzie's again. Her tongue played lazily with Izzie's. She gently sucked Izzie's bottom lip.

"Damn. That was sexy. I've been thinking about doing that all day. Come shower with me so I can do it again."

A whimper escaped Izzie. She wouldn't make it. When Anna left, it would fucking kill her. She wasn't ready to lose this.

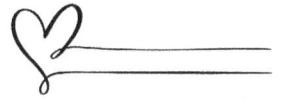

In nothing but a t-shirt and panties, Izzie looked sexy as fuck with her wet hair and satisfied expression. The wet locks soaked the shirt, making it cling to her bare breasts beneath. It was distracting as hell. They had played in the shower, but Anna still wanted more. Her pussy throbbed with desire. Unfortunately, they had some serious shit to talk about. She had gotten Izzie half nude for a reason other than Anna's inability to keep her hands off her. Anna didn't want Izzie to run when they discussed what their future would look like now. Still, she made Anna weak.

Anna straddled Izzie and dipped her head, sucking Izzie's nipple through the thin t-shirt. "Mine. So fucking hot."

Izzie took a ragged-sounding breath. She squeezed Anna's ass. "You're killing me. This is all the clothes I have here."

"Then let me have them. I'll throw them in the washer." Izzie really wouldn't get away then.

"I thought you wanted to talk."

With a sigh, Anna sat back on her heels. She didn't free Izzie. Izzie looked too good between her thighs. "Ugh. I guess if I have to be the adult."

Izzie laughed. Her body shook in a way that didn't help matters. "I believe in you. You can be patient."

Probably, but Anna didn't want to be. "I guess." She climbed from Izzie's lap. "Do you want this last slice of pizza?"

The nearly empty pizza box still sat open on the bed. Anna didn't want to accidentally knock it on the floor the next time she jumped Izzie.

Izzie shrugged. "We could split it."

Anna shook her head. "Nah. I'm good." She passed the slice to Izzie and set the box on the bedside table.

With her back against the headboard, Izzie ate. She looked like a Greek goddess. It was distracting. Anna supposed she couldn't put this off forever.

"After interviewing with Ron the second time, he wanted to talk again over dinner."

Izzie snapped to attention, looking like she wanted to scratch someone's eyes out.

Anna kept talking, so she didn't explode. "I thought he was hitting on me, and it was obvious he saw that thought hit me. He fell into babbling, explaining he wasn't asking me for a date. There was an agent friend of his that he wanted me to meet. He said I would be wasting myself on a local TV station. So I cautiously agreed to go."

"I'm sure you could probably take down three grown men if you had to. You were safe."

Damn. She really made Anna feel like she was a hundred times more of everything than she actually was. How could Anna resist her? She swiped her hand up Izzie's thigh.

"Maybe, but I still only agreed to meet with them in a highly public setting. It turned out to be fine, obviously. The agent, Kieran, is pretty well known. If I had known that was who he wanted me to meet, I probably would've freaked the fuck out. Anyhow, Ron ended up leaving early so his wife wouldn't worry. Kieran called a connection of his, and the next thing I knew, I was on the phone with the owner of one of the biggest sports networks around. With nothing but Kieran's recommendation, I had a job offer."

Izzie polished off her pizza and took a drink before responding. "That's wonderful and really nice of him. He must've been impressed."

Anna laughed. "Actually, he called me a shark."

Izzie's eyes widened comically, making Anna laugh. "You're joking. What an ass."

Anna laughed harder. "Not really. He's right. When I want something, I don't hold back. You should know that."

Izzie blushed in a way that Anna couldn't resist.

Anna pressed on before she threw talking out the window, and this was important. She needed Izzie to know Anna would never hurt her. "He was a blunt guy, which I admire. Unfortunately, he immediately read me. He directly asked if I'm a lesbian."

"Oh, my God. What the hell? Why? What does it matter? How did he even come to that conclusion?"

Anna appreciated Izzie's outrage on her behalf. She squeezed her thigh to show it, but Anna hadn't been surprised. "It seems it does matter because I'm the pretty face people want on the sidelines and in the locker rooms. That fantasy is gone if I'm gay. Men talk to pretty women without hesitation, even while wearing towels. Maybe especially then, because you know men. They still think sending dick pics turns women on." They both rolled their eyes and then laughed at the mimicked expressions.

Izzie's smile fell way too quickly for Anna's heart. She visibly swallowed. Her gaze dropped to her lap. Anna practically felt the hurt radiating from her and how hard she tried to hide it. She stroked Anna's hand before linking fingers with her. "I guess that means no you and me, huh?" A sad smile touched her lips and fell away. She still didn't meet Anna's stare. "I guess I sort of knew that, but I wanted to hope there was a chance for us." Her chin lifted. Tears swam in her eyes, but they didn't fall. She held Anna's stare. "Meeting you has been the best thing that's happened to me. Not the best thing in a long time, but the best thing. Thank you." She blinked, and a tear ran down her cheek. "I want this for you. No matter what it costs me."

Anna's breath stuttered. The air felt heavy. She never wanted to see tears in Izzie's eyes, but she couldn't make this choice for Izzie. "Here's the thing. I don't want to lose you."

Hope filled Izzie's eyes, but she let Anna talk.

Anna took a steadying breath. "I'm angry with myself. Why did I wait so long to talk to you when I've wanted you since the first time I saw you? If I hadn't waited, maybe I would've stood a chance of you choosing me."

Izzie swiped her cheeks. "What do you mean?"

It got harder for Anna not to cry. "I don't want this to be over, but I can't ask you to hide. You deserve to be with someone who shouts it publicly. I would never actually hide you, not even once I start this career. But once I'm on this road, if I—" Anna's hand lifted and fell. She didn't even want to say the words. Anna couldn't say she would have to tell people they weren't a couple if asked directly.

"If you're publicly gay, then you won't go very far."

Anna felt the warm tears spill over her lashes. She swiped them away. "Kieran said it was more like it didn't matter if people speculated. But if I corroborated the rumors, it would likely kill my career before I even got started. In this day and age, it shouldn't matter, but in this case, it does." Anna couldn't stop there. She needed Izzie to know that was not what she wanted. "It's not fair for me to ask that of you." She held Izzie's stare. "But I really want to ask that of you."

Izzie looked away and stared into space. She looked like someone had just dropped the most shocking news of her life on her.

Anna felt like a terrible human. Selfish and just awful. "Don't agree." She wiped her cheeks again. "I hear myself. You should slap me." Anna sniffed, trying to call her emotions under control. She was every bit the shark Kieran accused her of being. How could she ask Izzie to pretend? More tears flowed without her permission.

Then Izzie was there. Anna found herself on her back with Izzie's body covering her. Their tongues gently played. The sweetness nearly broke Anna. Izzie's mouth moved lower. Anna could barely hang on to a coherent thought. She hurt, but Izzie also had her on fire. Her T-shirt disappeared. Izzie sucked Anna's nipple. Her expression was loving as hell. If Anna's throat got any tighter, she would die.

Izzie kissed a path down Anna's body, taking her panties with her along the way.

Anna's breathing turned shaky as Izzie's mouth covered her pussy. She licked her way between the folds and gently sucked. Anna's spine left the bed. Everything Izzie did was so soft. It drove Anna insane. Everything disappeared except the tongue on her clit. Izzie took no mercy. Every time Anna got close; Izzie changed positions. It took Anna a couple of times of this to realize Izzie did it on purpose. With her fingers buried inside Anna, there was no way she could miss each time Anna almost came.

Anna's hips lifted. She openly fucked Izzie's mouth. Anna stared down the line of her body and sucked air. Between her shower and the sweat, her hair stuck to her face. Anna didn't try swiping it away. All she cared about was the mouth eating her.

"Please? Your tongue feels too good. I can't take it."

Izzie swirled her clit perfect.

"Fuck. Like that. Eat it. Your mouth is fucking heaven."

Izzie made a sound—like she tasted the best meal she ever had.

Anna lost it. She held Izzie's hair and fucked her tongue. Her hips lifted and rocked.

Izzie gave her everything. She didn't let up or give Anna's clit a break. Her tongue perfectly stroked that button until Anna was a fucking mess.

Anna clenched around Izzie's fingers. She held her breath. One final swipe of Izzie's tongue sent her flying. Loud, rhythmic cries escaped her as she took Izzie's fingers. Words left her lips that were forgotten as quickly as she said them. Nothing existed but the waves pulsing through her channel. As Anna collapsed into a heap and Izzie kissed her pussy like saying goodbye to a friend, Anna thought her chest might cave. She was pretty sure she had met the other half of herself, and they were as good as over.

Chapter Five

To her shame, Izzie had left while Anna slept. She hadn't said a word or left a note. Izzie didn't return Anna's texts. She needed time to think. Izzie posted signs on the windows and slapped clearance stickers on various items. She had a realtor coming to talk to her about an auction. In the meantime, Izzie might as well try to sell some stuff. She had nothing else to do. Her plans to talk to her aunt about the book idea were on the back burner. Izzie questioned her future a little more every day. Anna's move made Izzie realize something huge. There was nothing keeping her here. Not really. Not anymore.

Back when Izzie had moved from California to Philly, she hadn't been as excited about the move as she let her brother believe. She adored her aunt, but California had been her home. But Shane had been seventeen at the time, and doing shady shit to support her. He still did shady shit to support her. But back then, she had thought she set him free of her. Now she was an adult, and she could go anywhere. Izzie could move back to California and find work there.

Maybe even open a new shop in a higher foot traffic area and be closer to her brother. The possibilities were endless.

Izzie stopped moving and stared into space. She could even move to New Orleans...if she wanted. They probably had good spots for a new store too.

"Would you like some help?"

Izzie's eyes fell closed when Anna's gorgeous voice cut through her daydreaming. Her throat swelled. Only God knew how badly she had wanted everything surrounding her. This shop. Anna.

She forced herself to take a breath. "There's not much to do, really. I was mostly just making the best of my time left, I guess."

"So you were serious about closing."

It hadn't been a question. Izzie didn't look her way. She listened as Anna trailed around the store.

"Yeah."

"You didn't tell me what you plan to do now."

Izzie clenched her fists, trying to stop the way her hands shook. She cleared her throat. "I don't know. I thought about going into business with my aunt. She always needs help at the bookstore. Another part of me thought maybe I should move back to California. I've always wanted to be closer to my brother." She shrugged, even though she doubted Anna looked her way. "The possibilities are endless, I suppose."

Anna's arms encircled her.

Izzie didn't jump in surprise the way she would have expected. She couldn't explain it. It was like it was so natural for Anna to hold her that she simply melted into her place in the world.

"The other night, I didn't get a chance to ask what I wanted to. How about a third choice? Move to New Orleans with me. This new job comes with great pay. We could probably find a pretty nice place to live." She kissed Izzie's neck.

Izzie's heart raced for a million reasons. But mostly because Anna wanted her to go with her. "You want me to live with you?"

She felt Anna's lips shape into a smile against her skin. "Yes."

"Are you sure? I thought you wanted to hide."

Anna's arms tightened around her. "I never said that. It's more of a don't ask, don't tell situation. I would never hide you. There's absolutely nothing that would make me step back into the closet or pretend you're not mine."

Izzie couldn't stop her smile. Anna said Izzie was hers. She supposed countless military officers had lived the way Anna offered for years before laws changed. Did she want to watch Anna leave? Was Izzie that big of a coward? Was not saying the words publicly so important she would give up this thing that felt so right?

"Are we really going to do the whole stereotypical lesbian thing of immediately getting a U-Haul and adopting a bunch of pets?" Even Izzie heard the laughter in her voice.

"If that's a yes, then yes. That's exactly what we're doing." Everything inside Izzie roared to life. It was possible this would be the biggest mistake of her life. She didn't intend to let that stop her.

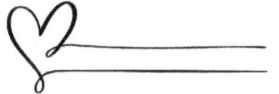

Anna had never held her breath so hard. She had put everything on the line by coming here. After waking up alone and having all her texts ignored, Anna had known in her heart Izzie was done with her. But she had to try, or Anna would regret it for the rest of her life. She one hundred percent believed they were meant to be. Anna knew in her gut, if Izzie said yes, everything would fall into place for their future. Everything would be okay.

"I've always wanted a dog."

Anna's eyes fell closed at Izzie's words. She was closer to tears than she liked. Her voice would barely work above a whisper, and it sounded shaky. "I swear I'll keep you happy. You won't regret me."

"There was never a chance of that." Izzie turned in her arms. The sincerity in her eyes stole Anna's breath. "Even if you left and never spoke to me again, I wouldn't have lamented over a second I've had with you."

"Same."

Izzie stole a sweet kiss. "We have so much to do."

"Oh my, God. So much."

Izzie shook with laughter.

Anna loved the way that felt against her skin.

"Let me help you get these clearance stickers on everything. The quicker everything sells, the better."

Izzie took a step back. "Agreed." She handed Anna half her signs and told her where to start.

Anna went to work. It was hard to watch Izzie putting her dream on clearance. She would find a way to help. Izzie had chosen her. Anna would make damn sure she kept Izzie happy.

Izzie flashed her smile, reminding Anna exactly why she was so hell bent to keep her. She was falling in love with that smile. Anna wanted to see it for the rest of her life. She would be damned if she never found out how far they could go.

Chapter Six

PEOPLE FILLED THE STREET asshole to
elbow on the Riverwalk to watch the
fireworks over the Mississippi River.
Fourth of July in the French Quarter
was a massive affair set to patriotic
music. They had only lived here for
six weeks and already Anna felt at
home. While she was used to moving
around the country from her time in
the service, she knew it was Izzie.
Izzie made every place a home.

Anna held her hand, trying her best not to lose Izzie in the crowd. She finally spotted a place to stand where they could breathe. A couple of homeless men lingered nearby, making most people steer clear. Izzie had some sort of strange repertoire with the unhoused. Anna imagined she had a ton of experience from owning a shop on Waterside, where there were also a lot of people living on the streets.

Anna simply stood aside and watched Izzie work her charm until it was like they had their own personal guards. She wasn't the type to judge. Everyone was much closer to homelessness than they ever were to being rich. It could happen to anyone.

Anna was still more than a little relieved to have Izzie's attention back. She was spoiled like that.

"Do you think the dogs will be okay? I feel guilty leaving them, knowing the fireworks will probably scare them."

It wasn't the first time Izzie had mentioned leaving their two rescues. Anna kept trying to reassure her. "They have a sitter and anxiety meds. But if you want to go home, we can."

Izzie chewed her bottom lip and eyed the massive crowd. Finally, she met Anna's stare. "No. I can't imagine trying to wade our way through all these people in the opposite direction. Plus, your dad and cousin are joining us."

That reminded Anna. She pulled the AirTag from her pocket. "I hope this plan works. Otherwise, they made the side trip for nothing."

Her dad and cousin, Bronx, were military men. They were only in town for some military games thing that happened every year. She was excited to see them. Izzie, not so much. Other than quick FaceTimes, she had met none of Anna's family in person yet.

Izzie opened her mouth, to no doubt ask for the millionth time if Anna's family would accept her. Thankfully, two men appeared.

"There's my baby girl."

Anna beamed as her dad hugged her and kissed her forehead.

"There's my baby girl's baby girl."

Izzie laughed as her dad gave her the same hug and kiss. She didn't realize Anna's dad had never wanted sons, much less a son-in-law. All he had was brothers growing up, and he married a woman who had nothing but brothers. Those brothers had gone on to produce nothing but more boys. She had so many cousins, Anna hadn't met them all.

Anna hugged Bronx while trying to keep an eye on her dad while he talked to Izzie. She was all smiles.

"Sideline reporter, huh? That's amazing."

Anna nodded. Bronx had always been her favorite cousin. "Yeah. I'm determined not to fall on my face too hard."

Bronx laughed. His eyes glowed with happiness. He had always been a fun guy. "You've got this." His eyes slid Izzie's way and back again. "It looks like you've found a gorgeous woman to keep you grounded. Your dad looks charmed."

Anna glanced over. Sure enough, her dad looked ready to keep Izzie. Anna wasn't surprised. Izzie had something that drew people to her. Maybe it was just because she was genuinely nice, and people felt that immediately in her presence.

Anna pulled Bronx forward. "Izzie, this is my favorite cousin, Bronx. Bronx, Izzie."

Bronx laughed. "Listen to her buttering me up. She's just hoping I won't tell you anything embarrassing." He held his hand out. "It's nice to meet you."

Izzie shook the outstretched hand. "You too." Her eyes swam with mirth. "I'll corner you later and you can tell me all the stories."

Bronx looked Anna's way and winked. "Oh, she's a keeper."

"I know." Anna never lost her smile. She had a permanent grin since meeting Izzie.

The first fireworks lit up the sky, pulling all eyes that way. Suddenly, the noise was too loud to hear anything.

Izzie pressed her lips against Anna's ear. "Did that go well? I feel like it went well."

Anna wanted to laugh, but she didn't want Izzie to think she laughed at her. Instead, she pressed her lips against Izzie's ear. "Told you he would love you. My parents know I have good taste."

Izzie turned her head and stole a quick kiss. She was always like this in public since the move. Izzie never made a show of being with Anna in public. Anna hated it. She snagged Izzie's hand before she could put distance between them. Anna recognized how much this flawless woman had sacrificed. It was long overdue for her to say that.

She pressed her lips against Izzie's ear again. "I forgot to tell you before it got too loud. I love you."

Izzie's head turned so fast, she nearly took out Anna's nose. There was so much hope staring at Anna, it swelled her throat. "Really?"

Even over the noise, Anna heard the question. She rolled her eyes. "I mean, yeah. Shouldn't that be obvious by now?"

"I love you too."

Happiness soared through Anna. She couldn't wait to spend the rest of her life like this. Anna wouldn't allow Izzie to feel like a secret. She wasn't at work. Anna tugged Izzie close and claimed her lips. No one paid attention to them. They were just two people in love beneath the fireworks. Izzie lightly tugged her ponytail. "I'm going to fuck you so hard later."

Anna swore the surrounding explosions could be felt in her gut. That was always how Izzie made her feel. She had never been happier or more focused in her life. Anna would rock her fucking world. First, they had to put their dogs to bed.

Thanks for reading. If you enjoyed this book, and would like to read about Izzie's brother, Shane's book is *In Daddy's Care.*

About the Author

CHARITY PARKERSON IS
AN award-winning and
multi-published author with several
companies. Born with no filter from
her brain to her mouth, she decided
to take this odd quirk and insert
it in her characters. One of her
greatest loves is writing morally
gray characters. You'll find them
scattered throughout her hundreds of
titles.

*Nine-time Readers' Favorite Award Winner

*2015 Passionate Plume Award Finalist

*2013 Reviewers' Choice Award Winner

*2012 ARRA Finalist for Favorite Paranormal Romance

*Five-time winner of The Mistress of the Darkpath

Connect with her online:

*Sign up for her newsletter: https://bit.ly/charityparkersonnewsletter

*Join her readers' group on Facebook: http://bit.ly/CharitysTribe

*Website:
https://www.charityparkerson.com

*A list of her social media accounts and giveaways all in one place:
http://hy.page/charityparkerson